LEGO NINJAGO
Masters of Spinjitzu

PIRATES VS. NINJA

ADAPTED BY TRACEY WEST

ISBN 978-0-545-60800-8

12 11 10 9 8 7 6 5 4 3 2 1   13 14 15 16 17 18/0

Printed in the U.S.A.   40

First printing, August 2013

PATIENCE, LLOYD!

"*Hii-yah!* Fists of Fury!" Lloyd yelled, pounding his fist into Kai's palm.

Ninja Cole, Jay, Kai, and Zane were training Lloyd in their Ninjago City apartment. It had been their home since evil Lord Garmadon had stolen the *Destiny's Bounty*, their flying ship. But a kitchen was no place to train a ninja. Kai had to use oven mitts for gloves.

"Lloyd, you are late for your next lesson with Nya," said Sensei Wu.

"*Aw!* But when will I learn Spinjitzu?" Lloyd whined.

"Patience," Sensei Wu told him. "Your Spinjitzu will only be unlocked when the key is ready to be found."

Sighing, Lloyd went off to see Kai's sister, Nya, a samurai warrior.

Lloyd found Nya stroking the nose of a four-headed dragon. The great beast was sick.

"One day, he'll be yours," Nya said. "Ultra Dragon is meant for the Green Ninja to ride."

The dragon's four heads roared.

"Looks like he's feeling better," Lloyd said as the dragon flew off.

Lloyd was destined to become the legendary Green Ninja. Sensei Wu sent the ninja to find a better place to train him.

"These will transport you any place you want to go," Sensei said with a smile. "They are bus tokens!"

THE MEGA WEAPON'S POWER

Meanwhile, Lord Garmadon and his crew of Serpentine warriors flew high above Ninjago City aboard the *Destiny's Bounty*, the ancient pirate ship Garmadon had stolen from the ninja. He also had their magical Weapons. Combined, they formed the Mega Weapon.

Lord Garmadon only had one problem. He didn't know how the Weapon worked!

"We spotted something!" one of the crew members cried. He pointed to Ultra Dragon as it flew past the ship.

"Don't let him get away, you slithering idiots!" Garmadon yelled. He pointed the Weapon at the dragon. "Destroy!"

But the Weapon didn't do anything.

Garmadon stormed belowdecks. He pounded the Weapon on a table.

A secret door opened, and an old journal popped out. Lord Garmadon read the story of Captain Soto. The pirate and his crew had sailed the ship two hundred years before.

"This crew sounds like they knew how to handle a ship," Garmadon said. "I wish they were here to show these scaly idiots how it's done!"

Suddenly, the Mega Weapon began to sizzle and smoke.

"What is happening?" Lord Garmadon wailed. "It won't let me let go!"

Then he heard a voice overhead. "All hands on deck! I am Captain Soto!"

PIRATES ON BOARD

Lord Garmadon rushed to the deck. Captain Soto and his pirate crew had come to life! They waved their swords at the snakes.

"I asked for a better crew, and I got it," Lord Garmadon realized. "The Mega Weapon has the power to create!" But using it had left him very weak.

Captain Soto marched up to Lord Garmadon. "I be Captain Soto, Stealer of the Seas!" the pirate snarled. "We are taking back our ship."

Then he turned to his crew. "Lock him and all his reptilian friends in the brig!"

Lord Garmadon was too weak to fight back. The pirates locked him and the Serpentine warriors in the ship's jail.

On deck, Captain Soto discovered that his ship could fly.

"This is too good!" He chuckled as they flew toward Ninjago City. "Just wait till they get a load of us!"

FOLLOW THAT SHIP!

Back in the city, the ninja had found a new place to train: Grand Sensei Dareth's Mojo Dojo. But Dareth was no Sensei Wu.

"I am a karate machine," Dareth bragged. But when he tried to show off his skills, he just got tangled up.

The ninja got busy training Lloyd. Cole showed Lloyd how to break a stack of boards.

Bam! Lloyd broke the boards — and the floor, too!

"With this power, you must be careful," Sensei Wu warned. "You must control it before it controls you."

Then the ninja heard screams outside. The pirates were attacking the city!

"You must stay here," Zane told Lloyd. "Your powers are not ready yet."

A bus pulled up, and the ninja hopped on. "Follow that ship!" Kai told the driver.

DARETH WALKS THE PLANK

Grand Sensei Dareth wanted to impress the ninja. He jumped onto the pirate ship from a rooftop.

"Surrender, or face the brown ninja!" he cried.

"Pajama Man! Get him!" yelled Captain Soto.

Dareth's silly karate moves were no match for the pirates. They grabbed him and tied him up.

"Keep an eye out for any other masked Pajama People," Captain Soto told his crew.

Back in Ninjago City, Cole, Jay, Kai, and Zane knew that they needed disguises. They put on pirate costumes and sneaked onboard the floating ship.

Captain Soto was making Dareth walk the plank!

The ninja couldn't save Dareth. Captain Soto pushed him off the plank!

"Aaaaah!" Dareth screamed as he fell.

"Yee-hah!" Lloyd appeared, riding the Ultra Dragon! He swooped down from the sky. The dragon caught Dareth in one of its mouths.

WHO WILL WIN?

"Ninjago!" the four ninja yelled. They used Spinjitzu to transform into their ninja outfits.

Captain Soto looked confused. "More Pajama Men?"

"Ninja versus pirates," Kai said. "Who will win?"

Cole jumped across the deck. He used his scythe to slice the feather off Captain Soto's hat.

The battle had begun!

Three pirates surrounded Kai. He thrust his sword into the deck.

Whap! Whap! Whap! He grabbed the hilt and swung around, kicking the pirates away.

Another pirate charged at Zane. He held a sharp dagger in each hand.

Crack! Zane used his whip to send the pirate flying backward.

Kai and Cole fought off two pirates. Jay had an idea: He used his nunchuks to break open a gumball machine.

The gumballs spilled out onto the deck. *Splat!* The pirates tripped and fell down — and so did Kai and Cole.

"Oops!" Jay said.

A BARREL OF TROUBLE

"Ninjago!" Lloyd yelled. He jumped off the Ultra Dragon and landed on the pirate ship.

Captain Soto charged at Lloyd. Kai jumped between them.

"Lloyd! You're not supposed to be here!" Kai yelled. He stuffed Lloyd in a wooden barrel to keep him safe.

   With the barrel over his head, Lloyd couldn't
see where he was going. He accidentally
bumped into the lever that dropped the ship's
anchor.
   Then he bumped into Kai. Kai jumped on
top of the barrel, and they rolled across the
deck together.

Kai fell off the barrel . . . and fell off the ship!

"*Whoa!*" he screamed.

He grabbed on to the anchor dangling from the ship. He clung to it as the anchor tore up the streets of Ninjago City.

A SURPRISE RESCUE

Back on the *Destiny's Bounty*, Captain Soto attacked Lloyd's barrel.

"Ninjago!" Lloyd cried.

He began to spin, turning into a green tornado of energy. The barrel exploded into pieces.

"I just did Spinjitzu for the first time!" Lloyd cheered.

Down below, Kai and the anchor were about to slam into a gas truck. If they hit it, the explosion would rock Ninjago City.

Up on the ship . . . *bam!* Captain Soto hit Lloyd from behind.

Lloyd fell into the lever that worked the anchor. It pulled the anchor back up to the ship — just in time!

Lloyd powered up with Spinjitzu — but he couldn't control his new abilities. Sizzling green light knocked down the mast of the ship. It crashed onto the ninja, trapping them all.

"You lose, Pajama People," Captain Soto said with an evil grin. "Now you're walking the plank."

Boom! Boom! Boom! The ship began to shake. The pirates looked up, and saw a giant robot stomping toward them.

It was Nya, piloting her giant samurai robot! She picked up the big mast and knocked down the pirate crew. Then she jumped out, slid down the ship's sails, and landed on Captain Soto.

"Who wins between pirates and ninja?" Jay asked. "It's samurai!"

The Ninjago City police rounded up the pirates "That your ship?" an officer asked the ninja.

Lord Garmadon was flying away on the *Destiny's Bounty*. "You snooze, you lose!"

"Great," Jay sighed. "Lord Garmadon's back, and now he's got our ship?"

Cole mussed Lloyd's hair. "Well, at least we've got this little guy!"

Lloyd grinned. He couldn't wait until he could be the Green Ninja all the time!

AR NO: 160557

FICTION